THE STUPEFACTION

THE
STUPEFACTION

Diane Williams

Alfred A. Knopf   New York   1996

THIS IS A BORZOI BOOK
PUBLISHED BY ALFRED A. KNOPF, INC.

Acknowledgment is made to the following publications in
which these stories first appeared:
Alaska Quarterly Review   *American Letters
& Commentary*   *Antioch Review*   *Blood +
Aphorisms*   *Denver Quarterly*   *Exact Change
Yearbook*   *Gulf Coast*   *The Iowa Review*
Nobodaddies   *The Quarterly*   *The Santa Monica
Review*   *Transgressions: The Iowa Anthology of
Innovative Fiction*

ISBN 0-679-44186-7
LC 96075692

Manufactured in the United States of America
First Edition

Thank goodness

Contents

THE STUPEFACTION

An Opening Chat

I am glad he is this man here so that I can do a fuck with someone, but I am regarded as a better cocksucker. It is one of those lovely times when a crisis does not come as a surprise. That is how I feel. I am glad he is this man here so that I can suck his cock and lick it. This goes on a little longer. I understood everything up to that point. This goes on a little longer. This—this cock is swollen. The throbbing of this cock begins. I felt sorry about what he had to do to me.

After this time, I noticed that I was not the same again as I had once been. I was much more swollen when the doctor arrived.

"We will get you back—we will get you back to

where you were when you were feeling strong. Is that what you want?" the doctor asked.

"Yes. I want to feel strong again. I find that giving a blow job takes everything out of me," I said.

"Yes, that's true," the doctor said.

The doctor might believe that with a person of my age he may be blunt.

You would think that it could not last—his wanting to get straight to the point where something ceases to exist.

The Key to Happiness

It would have been very unlike me to be unenchanted very often. Once when the telephone was ringing when I returned home, I was not delighted. This is the way it is often now in my own home. I am so used to it—as if I were in that part of the world where when you are a visitor everything is so enchanting. The radio is not even on very loud. I have turned it off. I am full of contentment. Follow along with me if you are full of contentment also, because then you will be able to understand this. One day I went to a plumbing-supply store. I needed a new faucet for the kitchen sink. The clerks were eating pizza. It was lunchtime. Each customer had to wait at least a half hour before being attended to. I had to

wait. The waiting was exquisite, startling, passion-
ate, magical.

A Shrewd and
Cunning Authority

Such a day as Dorriet's is a reminder to the hopeful that one cannot be hurt in a devastating way, that life should be as endless as possible.

So I am very happy, thought Dorriet.

She is a poor, sick person who is very lonely.

Dorriet said, "Come on, Dorriet."

She talked softly, aloud, more than she realized—frequently. She did not often wish to keep any of her thoughts to herself—her tendency to try to persuade.

"Daddy! Daddy!" shrieked a little boy who was sitting next to her on the powerful city bus.

The buses are powerful.

"Come on!" said Dorriet. Her fingers tightened into fists. The father's statements to his child, coursing from him as flowing fountains would in such a

7

desert, had the depth, the clarity of vision which proved to Dorriet that he should be the boy's father—that he was hers.

She can stay in the lap of their luxury if she keeps her voice down.

The Everlasting Sippers

I sip the coffee almost stealthily while I wait.

Within my purview, the receptionist drinks something.

"Liz, darling!" the receptionist exclaims when she looks up. She says, "Would you like something more to drink while you wait?"

In my mind, there isn't anything in my mind until I know that I want more coffee with milk.

"Do you want more—" the receptionist asks, "coffee?" The receptionist is drinking something.

Mrs. Fox enters, drinking something.

"You want this?" The receptionist is waving a carafe of coffee at both of us. The receptionist's face is small and round. She seems to have a nervous tic in one eye, squints it unexpectedly several times. She is the most faithful picture of tenderness I can call forth.

At length I rise, saying, "I see nothing against that."

That night, after I bathe, I put on my sumptuous robe, brocade. I spoon raspberry sherbert into my mouth with a sherbert spoon. I drink wine from a fine glass. I take a piece of fruit in my hand, not to eat it, to gaze lovingly at it! It is made of stone. There is no problem here with reality. There should be no additional people here at all, doing things, causing problems, that are then solved.

The Power of Performance

They are my protectors, you know. This is my brilliant reasoning.

One of them cried out.

Bridget came bustling back in, rubbing her hands together. She tiptoed around. She was not herself.

I sprang to my feet, thinking of what I might say to her. What I often do is brag about what I have and about what I can do. Sometimes I do not give a reason for asking for what I want.

Some banging, some thumping had begun out in the hall.

Pots and pans were being batted around, or that was a lot of coughing that I was hearing.

I should have already explained that we are people who only live here. I am not even sure how many people are here!

I heard doors slamming after they all ambled out. Everyone went away. They were being quieter out in the hall.

For me, this is no longer only a matter of mere poundings, or vibrations, or cracking noises.

On one occasion, the pounding was so forceful that one of our antique clocks was pitched forward out away from off of the wall. The clock stopped and had to be put to rights again. I bet my boasting will damage the chandelier.

Customary noise can occur in thick clumps, all of which can be turned sideways.

The Blessing

I said so in the letter, but virtually anyone could have said so: *You will have everything you want. I don't want to get your hopes up and then disappoint you.*

He just loves me. I have a very bad temper.

I walk forward with the letter in my hand, wearing my black dress, which gently slaps at my legs as I walk forward. For about an hour, I wrote the letter with a dull lead pencil. On the envelope, in ink, dutifully, I wrote the name, the address. The stamp is a large black-and-green one.

Life is curious. I drink half a glass of water. In the corner of the room, rather, in the center of the room, nothing any longer attempts to sing a song, or, on the other hand, is listless, actually sick to death, and will not recover. But I don't mean this as an incitement to get you to go tell people that everything can turn out happy, wholesome, just wonderful.

One afternoon, when you are particularly tired, you sit down. You will be sitting down, or maybe it will be late in the evening, and you have missed your dinner, and you have missed your lunch, and you have missed out on your breakfast, too, and the weather is hot, so that you feel hot. It is an unhealthy climate, which is humid and stifling, and the air you breathe is unhealthy for you, and then, you obtain your heart's desire.

Many times a person seems fairly satisfied already but is so unsuspecting.

Eero

Tthe twwo pairrs off iddentical chairrs hadd been chosenn byy tthe ownners off tthe hhouse bbecause off tthe strengthh off theirr ccharacter. Thhe chairrs neverr beckonned tthe litttle girrls forr sitting.

Tthese wwere gennuine Eero Saarinen chaiirs— yyou musst takke mmy worrd forr itt—sttanding be- hindd thhe litttle girrls innside thhe hhouse, fromm wwhere tthe girrls stood tto watcch rrain beeat dowwn onn little apple trees, whichh treees hadd been plantedd byy thee owwners aas ann orrchard, delliberately, beccause tthey looked sso muchh aalike.

Sso thenn, bbecause itt wwas theirr gamme, onne girrl waas saaying, "Ddo whatt II ddo!" tto tthe otther, jjust thhe waay thhe trees seemed tto bee doiing.

Uppon thhe *wwhat* worrd off herr command, thhe otther girrl ssaid thhe *wwhat* alsso. Ttheir *wwhats* coveredd overr tthemselves, hhers and herrs, andd thhen thhe exxact saame thingg wwas happening tto ttheir *II doos,* whhich arrived—nno jokke—withh aa majjestic simmultaneity.

Att ourr housse, itt's ggoing onn—anny gamme off tormment—wee still doo itt.

EEEverywhere!

APPPPOLOGY: Itttt wouldddd hhhhave beeeen entirrrrely tooooo tirrrresome forrrr meeee, tttthe onnnne whhhho wrrrrote tttthis, orrrr ffffor anyyyyone whooooo rrrreads thissss, tttto havvvve hadddd toooo advvvvance thrrrrough thissss, assss thhhhrough ourrrr ollllld aggggge, alllll thhhhe waaaay throughhhh thissss, evennnn thoughhhh thatttt's ssss so obbbbviously thhhhe waaaay, wiiiith aaaa grimmmm conssssstancy, itttt shouldddd beeee dddddone.

The Idealist

Without much enthusiasm, he led me down the corridor and opened the door. He didn't have to say, "I'm the one who did that." I knew. I assume he has been places where he has seen beauty, has had some joy and adventures.

He stumbled. He fell down. I might have struck him, that's why.

People have to do so many things just to live their lives. He probably suffered from the fall, but he acted oddly lighthearted. I am tempted to guess why that is. I owe him an apology, but not if he is never angry with me.

How do other people who don't know each other very well count their blessings?

While I eat my hamburger, we leave our clothes on because we are very shy. We hardly know each other. We manage to copulate occasionally and to remain ill-qualified.

A Moment of Panic

I am not ecstatic about the flesh on her not-yet-womanly body, and her other arm is very much like her other one, and so on. However, none of her duties are undone, or need doing, or are duties which will soon need doing, which could be vexing. She has no dilemma evincing a religious principle. And, instead of a gang of people fucking her, or poking fun at her fat cunt lips, she has under her feet a luxuriant carpet. In addition, her laundry has been laundered by her, and now, in spite of itself, this laundry is soft and folded, or hanging languorously. Some of her bedclothes are trimmed with a frothy white trim, because people she has never met made a decision that that trim would be nice.

From her side of it, looking anywhere, everything is sunlit, entrancing.

But beyond this recognition, which is mine, not hers, there is this aroma, unsmelt yet by me, blowing around through the cool air here, coming along, mixed with some sudden large gusts of true love, which all you do—you want it?—is on weekends, you inhale it.

The Revenge

She sat in a chair and looked out a window to think sad thoughts and to weep. Everything she saw out the window was either richly gleaming or glittering, owing to a supernatural effect. But she was not unused to this. She unlocked the front door. An infinitude of catastrophes was, as usual, apace—even as she walked out to the road. The ground was mushy from a recent rain. Her mind was not changing. Her mind had not changed in years. Somebody's headlights were blinding her. Her idea of a pilgrimage or of a promenade excited her. She was stalking, going swiftly down the avenue. She arrives at a plausible solution for at least 8 percent of her woes. I know what she is thinking, and am envious of her. But I am shitting on it.

The Capture

It is cubed. It has to be good. She displays the cheese in glass bowls. The stewing chickens—they didn't lay eggs, and they got their heads chopped off. They are tough. The fryer, the Perdue, the capon—they are tender, is her verdict on them.

She sees the time of the day on the clock on her wall. For herself, she takes this advice: Ponder large answerable questions. Believe believable things. Her table is set. Pursuit and revenge are her plan. She is at her own table in the presence of herself. Now she is eternally there because of what I have said about her here. She is being restrained for her remainder. She is my hero.

O Rock!

I don't wish to be callous or unfeeling. Go out if you like, but don't expect anything, even if we find the packet.

Actually, it is a large padded envelope that the man she follows into the café drops onto the table, then proceeds to undo. He has to break its seal.

She drums her fingers on her chin, watching him.

Her heart beats heavily, for which she is repaid in kind.

A thousand years are accounted for as he turns it upside down, empties out a dime, a penny, a penny, a dime, a dime, a dime. He empties out Time because of her. I am paying attention. Do *you* have to?

I hate it when you're like this.

The Lost Sex

Mrs. Camish said, "I know you need milk."

Mr. Camish said, "Don't look so haggard!"

A policeman was at my front door, listening to every one of my lies.

He had always been trouble. He was only going to do a short errand. He said he was coming right back. He was only going out to get milk and marble cake.

Mrs. Camish said, "Would you, for the record, please state his given name?"

Mr. Camish said, "Yes, do, but keep it short, if you would."

The policeman got out his pad again.

I said, "The man who vanished, you mean?"

Monsters

Counting this time—and she is counting—Sheba has held the animal twice in her arms. The animal is not one of her belongings, but her sister is.

This is a woman's story. None of the men will like this.

Sheba has been returned from Munich, where she stayed at the Arabella Westpark Hotel at Garmisch-erstrasse 2. At the Heimeranplatz S-Bahn station, she has been rescued from considerable danger by Denis. He was in Munich on business, coincidentally. Denis had to let go an employee in Munich. Denis had to be a beast. In Munich, he didn't want to be.

Now, at 4 rue Cassette in Paris, Denis is in his home, with Sheba, and the cat, and the furniture.

Denis appears to be suffering, has on his overcoat indoors. He raps on the chair on which Sheba sits with the cat and says, "Why are you like this?" The cat is sphinxlike. Denis pauses to consider how any monster may have poise, originality, and charm, and occasionally enjoy a foray to an almost unforgettable, dismal finishing up.

That is when the cat makes a choice about what to do next, and the other two are inclined to.

Luxuries

In a fussy mood, she came home to me. Her arms were gold-looking and cold to the touch when I touched them. The house key she had used to get into my house has a loop of gold cord threaded through it. She slipped my house key into the pocket of my jacket.

Our lives, which are leading us toward the shiny, bright flower of death, are austere, but if she says so, here, she can have money and glamour, she can have it. She can smoke a cigarette, since her husband is not with her, nor her children, nor her boyfriend. She has followed me. The sights we might see through my windows are associated with the mysteries—animals, automobiles, not much more. I see a cloud gray auto. I see a rocket red auto. I see a jet black animal.

Lois Holway, of Superior Exteriors, called. But I said, "No, I am sorry. We are not interested."

I was too busy being overcome with vain delights to say more. True, too, there was nothing more to say to the Holway woman that would be as true as *I am afraid of you.*

The Guider of the Prick

She wanted Bill to obey her. She wanted that very much. When Bill came down out of the tree, his mother was a little afraid of him, but she said, "Good"—meaning, she was glad that he was back down.

Boy, she thought, is Bill ever a handsome boy. She flung her arms around Bill. Then she tested the skin on her own arm with her fingertips to see if it was still as soft as silk, and it was.

Would Bill's mother ever say to Bill, "You've done enough for me already"?

Bill gets angry now, as a grown man, when some woman guides his prick for its entry into her cunt hole.

But back to when Bill was the pluckiest little boy

in the world, sitting on a tree branch, and his mother had thrown a small rock at Bill, and his mother wept and Bill wept, too. Bill saw apology, sadness, and disbelief in his mother's face. In Bill's face, his mother saw ordinary crying going on.

This is what Bill looks like as of today: He is large and unkempt, with unruly dark hair and dark eyes. His mother is proud of him. He is the keeper of the flame.

Speech

Thank goodness I am deeply sincere, so I stopped laughing. He had dragged me along to this refined filth of a hotel, which aroused my truest false feeling. On the way to the hotel, he was staggering and I was. If my wish is at last coming true, he is going to spring on me something that will make me feel as helpless as a human being.

He'll hear about it now.

A joke he told me had interfered with our breathing. Two women, I don't know, across the street were being dragged into the same experience, too—by a joke, or by something such as a joke.

Maybe he has not figured out yet how much I wish to stiffly represent myself at coital functions as stiffly as I do here as I speak.

For Diane

Very early on, I had a vision of excellence and a sense of responsibility of monstrous proportions.

It is best if no one ever sees me again. (You will thank me.)

I will not go to see someone just because he or she is conveniently located.

And, if you do that thing again, evil people will be ruined completely. Good people will feel great. Springtime will span the year because that's my decision. Anyone who would have preferred some other season may feel a not-so-serious mistake has been made.

When the good people begin their lavish new life, they will be especially indebted to Ira, who will provide everyone with a set of easy instructions to follow so everything turns out all right for them. Oh, they will be indebted to Ira.

I used to see a lot of this one woman. Ira will take care of her, because I've had it up to *here*.

Now, do you understand?

Plural

There is this one where they all put their feet up or slouch, because of the decree.

The worst of this is now over for Irene. She can just relax.

The iridescent ribbon, which might be regarded as pure or perfected, is in her hand. Her knees were drawn up. Her arms were exerting enough of her power.

Maybe she drew her thighs closed. She has soft, thin skin. She is plump because she has been stuffed with pralines, which is the secret of her plumpness. She likes to eat sweets.

She touched her genitals, thinking wistfully that they were flawless.

They are at their succulent best—red and yellow, but still firm—and if the skin is tender, you do not need to peel them. You can have the butcher make a series of fine, shallow cuts on the surface.

The Transformation

An unpleasant light coats all of her submerged body. She bears this coloration also.

After her bath, she feels she is significant. She eats some biscuits. The leftover biscuit morsels she goes ahead and she scrapes off of her plate into the garbage can. The stain on her shoe is hot blue or has been caused by some hot glue. To tell you a lie, even about this last, would be such a waste of everybody's time.

When the woman asks her loving friend, "Are we having that falafel for dinner?" the knife that the woman has been containing vigorously gets playful and she stabs herself with it mercilessly. She is aroused. She urges herself to think of herself. She says to herself, "You must, you must think of yourself and no other." She says, "To tell you the truth, you are dead."

Truthfully speaking, the above marvel has been described irresponsibly, without any perception on my part as to the why, the wherefores, or even any of the heretofores, or even why I thought to make the whole thing up. And I am not sorry for it at all. You deserve everything you get, I am sure, even the crap you have to read, and of course, this fake woman hasn't died; she has just transformed herself into me: I am about five foot three. I am a woman. I am of royal blood and huge intellect and I enjoy myself immensely, *come hell or high water!*

It is not in her nature to feel the way I do.

Gods of the Earth at Home

Mr. Moody and I were standing still for the sight, mentioning the sight, leaning slightly, or touching each other.

The soda was fizzing and the redness and the whiteness of the soda were dull compared with the redness and the whiteness of a fine radish.

It was Mr. Moody's boy Jim who had danced in with his bottle of cherry soda, turning the bottle, which was capped, over and over, and shaking the bottle, and the boy was spinning and hopping.

Mrs. Brute deplored the champagne we were drinking. She is my invention. She is going to take care of Jim.

Our exceptional meal was served on the golden plates. The silverware was real silver. Mr. Moody's face flushed when he drew me to him. He touched my beautiful auburn hair and my rich black velvet jacket. I had removed my deep sable. He could not be restrained from embracing me in the full view of everybody.

I just kept saying yes. When he said what he said, I said yes yes yes yes. I say yes yes. I say my excitement is so great, so huge.

I heard Mr. Moody's respiration. I heard him sort of faintly groan as he does sometimes at the very thought of having to eat my twat.

My imagination tells me that for everything which is not rewarding during a day, a heavy price must be paid.

I hope all of this will turn out all right.

What if it did?

It did.

We should all be so pleased that for the time being we must abide with growing up, getting married, having servants, slaves, houses, holidays.

Desperately Trying to Lie Down

Sometimes you were held, fondled, commented upon, weren't you? Yet I was told that nobody else had ever wanted you or had even asked about you, that I was the first one who had asked about you. When I grasped at you, twisted you, I saw some strands of your hair, the rather imprecise sketch of your eye, the overwhelming importance of your eye, and one of your eyebrows desperately trying to lie down sweetly on your brow, and with this view in mind, your face is as composed as my vulva is. I would like to suggest that the smartest, the strongest, the most perfect person in the universe is my property.

I am the dark one, the short one, the thick one,

the coarse one, who is so unsatisfied with all of my suggestions.

You said, "Here, let me help you," and there was such a really happy expression on your face that you must have been happy.

I Am a Learned Person

My name is Valery Plum. There is something funny in that. I cannot presume how true to life I am. When I see myself combing my hair, I seem true to life. I am so starkly represented. I try to see through somebody else's eyes, which would be a remarkable view. This is the second day in a row I have tried; that's because I—I am really looking forward to it, because, even though I have no devoted friend—my newborn is pretty, my lips brightly colored, and there's plenty more of that where that came from.

Up the spiral staircase I go to get the baby, who is not big. Only on the inside, the walls of this tower are the color of a butter cookie. *Heh heh heh,* he's wailing. Under these conditions, nothing but children is so much better than custard or genius or fame.

This may be true or false, but here I am.

An entire formula for feeling good is fitting for someone like a bat out of hell like me who does not tolerate flying with any aches or pains.

Miss M. Murray quoted some ingredients in her own book, and a Mr. Trevor Furze confirmed the same in his own. One of their key ingredients is yummy, would make dogs bark. I go up and down the stairs with it in my mouth. It dangles.

I can make it leap up again.

Careful

We could hardly bear it when she arrived home un-
hurt. The situation had grown intolerable. A week or
so after that, we saw her again, still no accidents.
She's a young woman. Maybe sometime soon she
will be destroyed.

As a matter of fact, just now she is in some peril.
She is having a conversation.

Among her lady friends, her masters, her heirs, she
shouts, "Charming!" Her voice is high, thin, nasal.

Just before this, we had thought of calling out to
her to wait, but she was already waiting.

She had heard the sound of her own voice without
any assistance or advice.

What if we never see her again?

We have nothing for—we have no plans for—we have no ideas for your—we have no wish to make you—we are—we—feel no— Let's just say there are other people, other than her, that we could speak to. We need to match up our feelings to our ideas for them.

Yesterday, we found it charming—all that shooting the semen around that they do.

What Knowledge Is Most Worth Having?

"There you are, Diane," she says, "an omelette."

She sets it down in front of me.

What next?

If light is being shed here, you will know.

My theory is that there is a profound, a gumbo effect that proceeds from one's being anywhere within earshot of the mention of food as a plaything.

Do you ever treat restaurant personnel shabbily?

Beware.

Indeed, personnel in general—Beware, I think— yes, beware of personnel or of any of their friends or their family.

Diagnosis

All this business, it is such a relief, she thought, when she did stop to think, but when she did not stop to think, she felt heartbreaking cramping.

There is no evidence yet on his condition.

She stretched her arms out over her head. She was woozy, so that she might not have seen the cold light of day.

"You were right about nearly everything," she said. It was a shot in the dark.

"About what?" he asked her.

Hearing that, she really shot him with her real gun.

Unable to get a direct flight to safe haven, she had to pass through New York. In New York, her torn ligament was diagnosed and her leg was put into a cast.

And then, during one of his emotional outbursts, the chief hospital physician informed her that she also suffered from the effects of a massive myocardial infarct, as well as chronic uveitis, irreversible glaucoma, and thyrotoxicosis.

A More Detailed Account of This Is Out of the Question

At the time of crisis, this man has arrived. Anything more I describe might give the wrong impression about his perfect timing, but that's too bad—how he has just appeared on the floor, lying down; another time at the back door, entering; once when I was down on my knees. Another time, we stood on the stairs. Once when I was leaning against the drawer in which I keep the flatware, he was with me.

I wanted to moan with my delight. But it would have confused him, because he says, "Are we there yet?"—the only words he will say in reply to anything ever.

I have never seen such a dignified man as he is. He has a pained expression on his face. His breathing is labored breathing. When he reaches my cartographer's side, the fellow is awake, sitting up.

It is so easy to get a boyfriend. By the light of the sun, I watch them. I get used to watching what I should have. Repetition of this kind is not lulling.

The Fuck

The pungency, the mystery, the awesomeness of his idea was terrific. Mother of God—he actually had a cloth and a spray bottle of something, because he was dusting his truck. His truck was blocking up our street that we live on.

As I ran away from him, I shouted, "I am not try-ing to run away from you!" Brutally, I kicked what I decided was my own stone, and I found a limp walking stick—a dead tree branch, smooth, just the right height—after it was boring for me to be brutal.

Ferocious, hateful dogs, working as a team, barked at me.

What are the Williamses putting that up for? I wondered, when I turned my corner. Now, he was over there, in their yard, not looking at what he was doing with their swing set, speaking only to me, when I came along.

There was no mention of being ill or an illness mentioned which was of an extreme or of a debilitating nature. Pleasure was the centerpoint, sexual pleasure, fun, surprise, gamy delight—seldom—well, all right, *once!*—disgust. He did not express desire other than sexual, which he was confident he would gratify soon. He had no concern that any woman, man, girl, or boy would not be a good-enough provider for him, or could somehow disappoint him, or turn up incompetent. Beauty, intelligence, education, gentility, cleanliness, worldly success, a moral attitude—none of these he ever referred back to. No concern over betrayal, no money problem was expressed, and yet, even so, I behaved curtly. I behaved as if he had digressed.

The Grand Occasion

The doctor had his wife with him, who is of true noble birth. I could make a list of her qualities, but what could happen if I perpetually bring up the same subject, talk about it on and on and on and on and on?

Dr. Daring lit the candles. He said to me, "Calm down."

"Thank you for inviting me!" I said. "This is a party!"

The doctor's wife asked to go outside for a walk. She said to her husband, "I'll be all right." He poked her playfully with the spoon and then did it again.

I said, "I think there is a slight drizzle out there, but it's really nicer than I think it is."

She sighed. Then she gave me the name of her own worst enemy. Understandably, it was a pseudonym—or a pen name.

The Goal

"I want to use yours."

"Use any bathroom you want to," she said.

He said, "Oh, you are my friend!"

He put his hand between her legs. He said, "Come. Sit up here. Back—*back*—"

He mouthed her; he tongued her; he nosed her between her legs. He murmured, "Let go."

"Oh, that was a treat!" she said. She stood. She stood on tiptoe and she embraced him.

"I have to go to the bathroom," he said.

"Use the children's," she said.

He twisted to gaze at her while she was not straining to be anything more than what she is. He was free and happy, too. In her bathroom, she was reach-

ing to turn the little spinner, to twirl the screw pro-
peller which releases some of the water through the
bunghole into the remarkable.

My Reaction to Life

Our half-broken horses were rearing and whinnying, their blackened figures brutish and inhuman. Some of their rumps were being slapped.

I tore off my gloves. My hands were warm. Although, the largest single hot body among us, I bet, was Harry Winch's brown horse, Drifter. It is hard to describe these animals which are so stiff-necked.

I stroked my horse, told it to stand still. I can be indifferent and patient. I am one of those who keeps expecting the dark heart of human desire to be revealed to me.

Others were looking down into the gorge, with their mouths agape.

Chet Henry said, "Now what?" and there is no going back and changing what he said, because that is what he said. He is a man who may have temporarily gotten off of his horse so that he could be loved, or so that he could be hated, or so that he could hate me.

Now what? I am going to answer him the only way I know how. I said, "We're going back to the ranch." The ranch has real log buildings, cowboys, excellent meals.

Nobody has to tell me how we made it back through the thicket to the Ridn-Hy. The traveler in me is full of hope. She is a splendidly bland and a smug woman.

The Dirty Necklace

She used the bath mat to dry the wet necklace, and dirt from the necklace showed up on the bath mat. She could wash the necklace again. She put some bar soap on the necklace, not too much, and then she rinsed the necklace. She repeated this. The necklace could be washed again. The necklace could be scrubbed with a scrub brush. The necklace should soak overnight in a basin. She dried the necklace by rubbing it against the bath mat, so that more dirt showed up on the bath mat. She put the necklace on. She fingered the necklace and saw that its parts were cut glass, amber, or plastic. The necklace was meant to be hers. We do not know who else, if anyone, has ever worn the necklace. There are other necklaces which she owns—

not exactly the same—but these necklaces are a
series of misunderstandings—as is everything—at
your throat.

The Helpmeet

To my surprise, Diane Williams wants me to hold her fucking ass. I am an annoyance rather than a deep disturbance. In other words, I go to my room when I am told to, shut the door, and I stay there until I am given my permission to come out.

When I come back out, some secrecy is necessary. Nothing could have seemed more essential when I took off my peg-top trousers. I untied my shoes. Stood. I felt so tightly bound to her while we were stiffly rocking.

If I go away someday, I want to know how she will live without me.

I will ask her to go into detail about her sexual needs.

Why do I even care how many of her needs there are?

Just for conversation's sake, let's say there are just two.

The Masturbator

We are all so much the same—our size, our shapes, and we are perforated. I put my finger on a crack in my skin. I have been searching for one gesture of my own such as this which I can remember—return to, and return to, which could direct and give sense to my life. I had ignored other motions of my heavy body—the lowering and raising up of my hind end, which I often do. My legs are tired, and I feel weak-kneed, and it looks to me that there is a place to sit down to rest near a tree. This tree's trunk is a subtle tawny color. The ground is dark, has speckles. I press on my hand. I am still not uncertain what to think when I gently rub my hand, which seems to me dirt-free and oldfangled. There are much more up-to-date revealers of the truth.

Boiled and Starched

For the slow, tender people, for the tall people, for the fragrant ones in the shady locations, I use squill. Now, for the people in my hot, dry places, for the people who are essential to me, who grow easily— the interesting people who can help rid me of pests! the worthy people with their reddened eyes! the suitable people—what did I do to them?—the business was not apparently unforgettable.

The hall where these people had congregated was hot. Even Jimmie received a few hoary sticks of furniture—which are not from me, by the way.

My throat aches; my eyes fill with tears. The shock of my knowing every wish of theirs has come true has worn off.

Now I continue to the near side, along the lake. I

see the ruins, the storefronts. From the boat, I see the small chapel. On board the boat, I fall and bruise myself rather drastically.

I get off the boat and return by a conveyance along the thoroughfare I have used to reach all my hours in my days.

Okeydoke

The man lied is the best ingredient in my veal steak deluxe. I am going to vacation in the man lied. I never will the man lied for the third time.

I the man lied that that's wonderful and exciting and I look forward to it. He is telling me how many the man lied he has to have in a day.

I expected to the man lied blood.

The man lied, "I have never seen the man lied like that one."

On the man lied, when some chicken and a potato were roasting in my oven, I would not leave the man lied. I liked to tell the man lied how many orgasms I had in a day.

The man lied was sure I was hearing a waterfall. But what I heard was the grinding of the man lied.

The Fuss

First of all, I do not want to keep the thing a secret, because they were not doing any harm, I assure you. They ate. They drank heartily. They threw stones which sank into the sea. They jumped into the sea. We followed them. The sea was bright and whirring. I was not used to being cold in the water. I am not used to keeping a secret, either, which I think is the best plan. It was a journey. There was a beautiful sky. We were too cold creeping under it. A little farther on, they marched. I cannot form an idea from this.

Thank You

A margay has heavy black eyebrows, heavy, black, wavy hair. An ocelot is very much the same. No margay has been seen around here, but we were determined to find one if it is in the books. We crouched in a field studded with hares and cows and dogs. We were in extreme agony because we were bewildered and we had been wandering. (I was in a very bad mood.) Several of us have long, gray, matted hair and are extremely ugly. I wear a black skullcap. An odd-looking stranger (but what stranger isn't?) hobbled up to us and told us what to do. She squatted. Her knees bumped into her shoulders. She told me to think about something else for a change.

The Purpose

This is better than what I had last year. People are happy for us. They are happy for both of us. I said that I am content to have very little. I could want more if other people would just tell me what I need.

I cough. I do not like my spaghetti. I ask for another cola drink, could I have one more.

I am told, however, "No!"

Every now and then for me, cola can be cold and abundant, its scent not objectionable. It is not fragile or flat, or well chosen, well placed enough to serve the exact same purpose as she does for me.

She was everything she said she would be.

I am noticing an outcome when even an indescribable force can change a fact.

To herself, she said, "I put too much of this on."

Even if not one interesting idea occurs to me, I also have something I could say which I would like to say about my opinion that my ideas give me something to talk about.

Could I have one more?

I said, "Have one of these."

I was told, however, "Not on your life!"

The Primary Intuition

We have conspicuous yet, I think, respectable hair on
our heads. Even so, my son and I could scare people.
We have. We walk along. I see scarlet-fruited, big-
leaf winter creeper, inkberries. At last, we arrive at
the village. I knew what we would do, where I would
accompany him.

Pierre and Esther, our enemies, entered a shop. I
had seen Esther, with her trailing spray, wearing her
sautoir, open the door. The light spreading rapidly
from the shop windows was not warm and inviting.

We had the advantage of staying close to the
building.

By the time we left town, I had an invisible ring on
my finger, as well as a strong brown cut, which has

the appearance of an aeriel rootlet. I had watched my son drink from a swaying glass of juice, which is perfumed, forms in clusters, turns yellow, before it comes into sight.

Rain

Found stretched out dead, dead, dead is a speck that used to look like all of the rest. I don't say they're all alike, but I might as well say that. Perhaps my mother said that a speck with its hairs gone, all full and wet, cannot be fierce.

One fine morning, I wasn't so loquacious. I was feeling unwell. When I recovered, I saw a speck roving on myself. I struck it, squeezed it with some warmth. Perhaps my father encouraged this. Perhaps, without my shoes on, without my stockings on, I liked to deliver a blow. I felt eager to command myself to not get further acquainted, to break away by force from specks. Perhaps my brother paid attention to this Rachel Higgins who was gliding along.

The Festival

I put your trousers on, but in your opinion, I should not have. Their chief value is decorative. Then I went back, had another look at the woman.

I put pillows under her head.

I don't just sit around, either, and why? I am surprised that they didn't tell you about me, that I had a good upbringing!

How much fun I had with my prick up inside of the great Diane Williams. She held the tip of the prick firmly. She is pleased to feel.

I know that whatever I might decide to do, it could be what you might do!

It's just happening sooner! For more than for four years! Go on in, see Diane. I was told that all sorts of people are in her room. She opens her legs this way. You must avoid the decay at her stem's end.

Yet joy is memorable, cutie! And, when this holiday begins, it is twice as rewarding as pain is.

The Builder

I drank dark water, later on, afterward. I urinated, emitted gas. I was pleased, tired, had cramps. I could not stop the monster from causing its destruction. It had left no real damage after the cleanup. Out of devotion? Because of fear? Or pride? I often have an outburst of my free will. I know what I will do if I have sexual intercourse, how I am going to hump and plan. I suspect many others need to plan your sexual intercourse.

The Answer to the Question

A coil of green, a part of me, or any additional garnishing, when assembled, can produce sufficient allure anyplace.

The old idea that enticements should be ever more sophisticated is what prevents most seers—plumbers and electricians alike—from being optimistic.

Keep on hand containers which you have filled compactly. Wrap these securely. A stream or a flow is a thing of the past.

Their Privileges

Do not say there is no information about us. He had one leg in the air. My head was down.

Living can provide a sense that everything has already happened.

I have admired as many trees, as much shrubbery, as I could have. I am not lying. I have gone out of my way to say how grateful I am for shrubs, over and over. I know I spent enough time on that.

I never joked around with anyone. I don't think I have been very foolish.

Then it is my turn to sit and to think about what I will get.

Escapade

The most attractive designs in my life are covered over lightly with nuts.

On a weekday, I am getting smaller and smaller and some of the stories I tell are not true. Maybe it is merely an experience of happiness that I must try to endure.

I would do anything for you. I will be near you.

Am I smaller?

Am I small enough yet to be all filled with blood?

The Suitor

We are becoming persons who should, of course, be loved and honored. We become people who can do the impossible.

Was anyone surprised to see us take on a different shape and character? In the name of everything which is sacred, I can predict your fate to ensure that you will never worry.

I am your friend, if you do what I tell you to do. Don't worry.

Let's pretend I have made mistakes. Let's pretend that these sorts of mistakes are the ones I never should have made. I have no respect for you, for instance. I think I can just pick up anything of yours and look at it. I hear myself shout, "That's the trouble!"

The Strong Petals of Quiet

I saw the duster after the duster had bloomed. The duster leads me where I should go, encourages me. The duster advises me to lie down on the lawn to rest, takes me to the sweeper's shop on Gower Street, which is not in an uproar. The duster is my shepherd.

It comes toward me, to guide me on the darkening plane. I could show you how if you could see me on this peninsula.

I will never put the duster away from me.

THE
STUPEFACTION

One Place

Same Place

Everything

For

You

Is it necessary to state
a guarantee of my goodwill?

If they come in, they go
right back out again.

—SEVERAL OF MY NEIGHBORS

1

OH, I HOPE YOU LIKE
EVERYTHING I SAY!

Somewhat embarrassed, he would not admit that he wanted to do something with her right away which might surprise her or possibly cause her some pain.

"I came directly here!" he said. His sad expression had vanished. He said, "Let's go!"

They did not take her little dog with them. It is dangerous to show her dog too much affection, she believes. This could cause harm.

She had another one of her own ideas when she saw a pool of some forgotten water, when she saw some of the forsaken hills. She said, "This is the nicest part of the trip!"

More of her own ideas occurred to her when they were up in the hills.

If she is not much different than I am, she was hoping I would like everything she would say.

He frowned. He said, "We must hurry." He said, "Go on ahead."

By this time, it was twilight. They could barely see the ground or the form of a person doing something patiently and carefully. This apparition is what she has so often feared. She said, "I think that that looks real."

They were struggling. He said, "I'm not sure I like this whole thing. Can't you hurry?"

2

THIS HEAVENLY LIFE IS NOT
FORBIDDEN

I'll try," she said.

She felt the need to urinate.

They crossed the bridge on foot, and they entered the woods.

This heavenly life is not forbidden.

"We don't know a thing about these woods," she said. "It is heavenly." She sighed, wondering about his bobbing cock.

Something else crawled away and hid under a log. Something else brushed his side. She had had to shoo them off.

He begged her to let him keep on talking.

He likes it when she is acting as if she is nice and friendly, when he is imagining he wants to be with nobody else.

Amazingly, they did not lose their way in the

woods. Yet neither of them had the ornament that wards off evil and that could bring either of them good luck.

When she squatted down to urinate behind a tree, she listened to her noise. A trickle of her urine wet one of her shoes. She had a tissue with her so that she could wipe off her shoe that had been wetted.

Once in the course of her entire lifetime, she almost saw where that urine of hers pours out from.

But no, sorry, she never did actually exactly see.

She was summoning more pleasure when she heard the squirrels.

These squirrels are so fidgety. A few of these squirrels were becoming violently ill and would have very little privacy when this was the case.

Meanwhile, far away, in her garden, her dog was chewing on a rosy green pear that he held between his paws, and not at all tenderly. The dog was gnawing, biting, on the pear as if it were his own flesh and blood!

In the evening, she put her hand down inside her blouse and there between her breasts there was a little something which she would set free.

3

IT WAS A JOYFUL TIME

She pulled out the honest soul but did not examine it before she tossed it away.

It was a joyful time.

Soon she had a fire going in the fireplace.

They have located this ideal cottage. This cottage has been created to augment, to ease an intimate relation, to provide long-lasting help, to reduce the possibility of sin. She will never be one of those people who is slain.

He's probably happy. He is probably happy.

He has something in his hand.

She is trying to give herself something more to be grateful for than only just some spasms up inside of her cunt. Oh, I love this! she must be saying.

She is hoping to understand anything.

She'd like to tell him, Stay there where I put you.

He was opening the drawers—drawer after drawer.

The cottage had been prepared for them, or so it seemed to them—firewood in a basket, a packet of matches, common white spring blossoms in a vase, soap, towels, food, clean bedding—everything!—even a freshly laundered blue terry-cloth robe was there! Before long, the cottage has lost its chill.

She followed him into the kitchen and watched him open a cupboard door.

A surprise clattered.

4

CAUTIOUSLY, SHE LOOKED AROUND

She did not remain calm. "I think you've done enough searching!" she exclaimed.

He believed that everything was so cosy. Soon enough, there was the fragrance of cream.

In the kitchen, she had prepared a full-fledged cocoa bread pudding.

An insect drifted up before her eyes, then flew away. She briefly inspected the ether for the insect. Then she looked for a miracle of beauty high up in the air in the out-of-doors.

He lit beeswax candles—dripless, clean-burning— which produced soft light.

"That's ours!" he said when she found a jar of red jam. She saw him steadily stride. She thought, I know I can trust him.

Orange sparks sprang up the way they usually do when he interfered with the fire.

On the hearth was a pair of lady's dancing slippers, of delicate dark velvet, covered by gold embroidery and braid and daisy patterns made of ivory-colored small pearls, as well as a pair of man-sized, wide-topped, funnel-shaped half boots of embroidered leather.

Offering him his pudding, she said, "This is so cosy!"

These are people who are often alone together. Perhaps they could be cruel, useless people, incapable of understanding very much about anything.

Cautiously, she looked around.

This may be a trap.

5

DON'T START IMAGINING THINGS

Don't start imagining things," he said while he was slumped, eating his dessert, in the chair, his trousers lowered to his ankles. "This is so cosy," he said. He believed that he had thought of the idea of cosiness all by himself.

"It is eerie, though," she said.

Contents of the drawers were scattered on the floor.

He chuckled.

She did not ask for an explanation, such as, What amuses you? She never ever wants to be the kind of woman who causes him to be cross, who speaks harshly to him.

Just as she was attempting to handle another one of her concerns, the telephone rang. She had forgotten about sexual pleasure. The ringing reminded her.

When the telephone was ringing, he said, "Uh-oh!"

She grabbed his arm and then she guided him through the cottage. He was using his knees to hold up his flapping trousers. She was behind him, her hands on either side of his waist. "In here," she said powerfully, flinging the door open, pushing him forward.

6

SHE PUT THE LID OF THE TOILET IN PLACE

D on't do that," he said.

After all, he had invited her to come with him because he had thought that he might have some fun.

If the telephone rings and rings, or if there is knocking at the door, this is alarming. The telephone is an obdurate potentiality.

When he was stepping into the bathtub, which was brimming with the same sort of water she is accustomed to, she worried.

What should I do? I should do something, she fretted.

He made no comment. She did not see his face. She was not at all certain that she was in fact supposed to lightly touch him in this circumstance, or to grip him otherwise.

She put the lid of the toilet in place, then she watched him from her perch on the toilet lid.

In this same room, she had earlier moaned, "What am I going to do?"

She is just here to make herself happy.

"I want to touch you," she said.

"Fine," he said. "Do it wherever you want."

She put her finger on the tip of his penis and she pushed it down. She bent his penis.

"Can I kiss you?" she asked.

"Fine," he answered.

So she did.

She kissed his brow; then she petted the top of his head.

"Do you want me to stop?" she asked.

"No," he said.

He said no.

7

SHE WAS ALERT TO HER TERROR

She kissed his waxy pate many times.

"Oh," he said, sighing, "where did you learn to do that?"

She was sure she should not answer this question. This is the oldest, the most difficult, question.

Meanwhile, the night advanced. This had been confirmed when she was sitting on the rim of the bathtub, since she could then see out the window.

She was alert to her terror but was only faintly informed of her total helplessness.

His knees were up near his chin. He looked so handsome to her naked.

She flinched when he spoke. She did not know what to say, so she is quiet. She had nothing to offer that might reveal the secret meaning of things—the truest things.

It is easy to forget that during the next two days she solved the only problem that remained for her to solve, at which time she did say, "I thought of that all by myself!"

If anyone had entered the room, such a person might have been curious. Probably at times he had wondered, What is the matter with us?

Her interest in teasing him startled her.

"Oh, yes, I want to," she said.

8

SHE APPRECIATED IT SO MUCH WHENEVER HE TRIED TO PLEASE HER

Earnestly, he kept on having these sexual sensations.

He was feeling better, although he was still afraid of being scolded.

When he got up out of the tub of water, he predicted some horse sense, some magic, and some wishful thinking.

She asked, "Are you going to get into that bed with me?"

He answered yes, that he was.

Since she knows in general what to do, she did not feel ill-tempered, even though her first efforts to please him usually did not work.

She appreciated it so much whenever he tried to please her.

When he gleefully played with her, this might not have been a dream.

He did not remember that he had not done anything of this kind in a very long time.

He is so weary of trying to remember anything, because prior to this escape from his life, his life had been one of the most wearying lives ever lived. Presumably, his life had occasioned a type of slave labor.

He said, "I bet nobody has ever done this!"

"I don't know," she said. "Just stick it in and I will think about it."

9

SHE WAS SOILED—BUT WETTED?

The accounts of how she lost her dignity vary. She does not know that she is vehemently inclined to be made happy at any cost.

Force it on me, she is craving, and please forgive me for anything I could ever do that is wrong or that I have already done that is wrong, and forgive me for what I am doing right now!

She is slack-faced, flushed, after that. She has a sense of a heartening achievement.

"That's it, my darling," he said. "If I were your mother, I could not be prouder of you."

To her surprise, when she was not asleep, he reached out and insinuated his arm around her!

Late that night, water is running. He must have been getting into the bathtub again. Oh, the nice bathroom.

Remember, nothing really terrible is ever supposed to happen to her.

She was soiled—but wetted?

She was the only person she had ever heard of she could envy.

About half an hour later, he approached her. His purpose was to kiss her lovingly. He said her name sweetly, which caused her to feel very fortunate.

Perhaps this should have been brooded over—what her name is.

Her eyes, ears, nostrils, mouth, anus, legs, and other parts of her are wrongly formed.

Her skin is extraworn, extrafaded, extraunfirm. Her character, her intellect, her health are relevant but not known now.

He is the same size she is, or he is much smaller than she is. His skin is so different from hers.

He is gentle. He is nervy, but this is not all that he is.

10

OUTSIDE, EVERYTHING IS
SPECTACULAR

He is terrific.

His robe is something I have worn. It is a deep dark blue robe, rude, but not handmade. If someone were to take his robe seriously, his robe might appear to be ongoing, as if this terry-cloth robe could stand up to the test of time, or to the open air.

Outside, everything is spectacular.

Inside, the man and the woman chat a little, laugh quite a bit. They may question each other. Also, they answer each other. They can be sexually pleased. They bathe. The man cleans the kitchen floor more carefully than he has ever cleaned himself.

At this point, far, far away, the woman's everlasting dog cannot remember how he used to pity himself.

Her dog will not be lonely. There cannot be another plan other than this plan for her dog's future.

The dog considers himself superior to other dogs.

Other creatures could be accounted for as well, with vulgar praise, or there will be public disappointments.

The question is, What more should this man and this woman do there in that house? All of the usual methods of sexual intercourse can be delightful, especially if done with care.

Behold! The man is going to give the woman something!

It is a ruby ring, which fits her, with a single ruby as shiny as mine is, which he discovered in a cake pan—and he gave it to her.

Imagine! The woman can hear the splashing and the rippling of the light inside the gem!

She groans. She shrieks.

This ruby has been dripping with blood once upon a time!

The woman takes a puff of the man's hair in her hand when she says to him, "Oh, thank you!"

Oh, why did I ever let her into the cottage? Was it because she is prayerful?

11

SHE IS NICE, BUT SHE HAS AGED

She is nice, but she has aged. Now she is pulling her blouse about her. But she is not sad.

I think there is a storm outside—wind and rain. Dirt is blowing into the cottage from under the windowsills. The amount of dirt, the power of the wind, is a bit of a shock to me.

A lot of age-old dust is turning itself into black water around here.

The man's palm is on a windowpane. So is his nose, until he notices that it is.

My worrying about this will not be helpful.

12

HE SAID, "LOOK OVER HERE!"

To him, the most enthralling prospect is the most satisfying. He said, "Look over here!" He motioned for her to come closer. "Come over here!" he said.

To her, of course.

The moment has now arrived.

Now, for an excellent moment, they are both gazing at the murk. He is a brave man.

"What is it? What is it? What is it?" she begged of him. "Will you answer a question?"

Once he exclaimed, "What is this?"

They both saw what they should see.

When did this exertion of their vision ever take place?

It took place as my spirit soared, when I observed that they did not want to look at each other.

There was the scent of a charred lamb chop, but there was no indecency in this fact, either.

I saw a sign of some life—and luxuriant shadows—when the door blew open. It was a body with a slender neck, a darting head.

13

I SAW IT ENTERING

I saw it was dressed.

The man raised his voice, nearly lost his reason crying out to it, but no answering voice came back to him.

It was necessary now for me to be reassuring. Every moment still counted. I was curious, too, and I was intrigued by the suddenness of its entry. But I was certain we were all still safe here.

A sound not unlike castanets started up. Then, as things will, it stopped.

Within less than an hour, I promise you, this visitor was capable of feelings and was yearning to steal back to its own people.

The man screwed up his courage. He went up to it boldly. This is what I want to do.

The newcomer was so close, I could have touched it. The face of it was somewhat adorable.

Sometimes I heard gasping, or a heavy footfall, which could not have lasted for more than for a few instants.

In my opinion, this creature had stumbled into a trap.

14

YOU SHOULD HAVE SEEN WHAT I SAW

Its profile is remarkably like my mother's.

You should have seen what I saw, for this thing was not much larger than you could manage to see.

The man went to clutching at it. He was trying to hold on to whatever he could, to take it into his hands.

At first, all that he could see was a vague shimmering, which he could have been undone by. Yet, the older, the stronger, we are, I think, the greater our sense of wonder.

The woman saw it appear when the dearie's hands were held above the head—then again when it was folding its palms together, trying to keep its chin up.

15

IT WAS A GOLDEN STRUCTURE

I knew that I would have to make proper use of this radiance. It was a golden structure—brighter than any of my daydreams.

With my step-by-step intervention, especially that all concerned should keep on breathing in their fashion, I tell you that the woman thought to place in front of it a small dish of condiment.

"I think I'll sample a bit of this," it said.

Oh—but oh, oh, oh.

Choking, having done so, it declared, "I have been killed."

16

HE SAID, "LOOK! HERE'S SOMETHING! THIS MAY BE VALUABLE!"

A little of that goes a long way," the man said. He gave it something to drink.

"Have a glass of this," he said.

And eventually this substance proved to be soothing.

Mentioning that it would return again soon, this dream come true was able to disappear gracefully back into its origin, but not before the three of them had achieved a certain sense of society with one another.

And while it had seemed that the darling had actually put the toxin into its mouth, in fact, this had not been the case.

By the time I had forgotten about the interruption, the old house seemed snug again to me.

I could see clearly the faces of the man and the woman—because I needed to.

He had found a few more treasures.

Some of the bracelets are huge.

He was whispering—but he was not whispering to me!—"How's my darling?"

He was unbuttoning, unzipping, pushing everything down.

When he throws his arms around the woman, he does not know when to let go of her, so that he has to guess when he should.

He should never know absolutely.

So far, he has made some correct judgments, which it will never be possible for him to forget.

He has not washed up any of their dishes or attacked any of the more puzzling tasks.

Nearly everything he ever does gives me a lewd thrill.

He was taking off the woman's old shoes, even though she was telling him, "I'll take it off." They are the kind with laminated leather inserts and fabric laces.

You know.

17

"DO YOU WANT TO HELP?" SHE ASKED

She is behaving as if she is a pleasant woman.
She says, "There is a way you can help me."
He is frightened when she tells him how to do this.
He said, "Oh, no, not this time!"
Who would have thought he would be braver than he usually is?

He goes back along a corridor into the bathroom, and she follows him. They are just like ordinary people—and it's not funny!

They must show each other their real shapes, their true skin. They have to.

I am impressed by what lies in store for them, which includes this current adventure of theirs, as well as another expedition.

She washes herself. She combs her hair. She may be deeply in love, as well. I think she is so beautiful.

Oh my God! He is emptying his bowel into the toilet right before our very eyes! But in spite of everything, it is really worth it to him! He has a strong, well-controlled method of defecating.

This event has gotten her strangely worked up.

Let me say that the scent of this man is fantastic, distinctive! It is nutty and sweet.

The linens—the towels in the bathroom—are not stained! There is a blot of something awful in the sink.

He asks, "You look sad. Are you sad?"

18

HE SAID, "OH, NO, NOT THIS TIME!"

She is not sad.

She is nice.

At some point soon, she will be down on her back, with her knees up against her tits.

The man tries to remember what to do next.

"Don't forget whose idea this was! It was my idea!" he says.

Nothing too fancy. That's the beauty of it!

"Are you afraid of something?" he asks.

She is afraid to think about what she is afraid of. She feels an urge which even I should not be at liberty to disclose.

All through the wild night, they expect the wind to be blowing.

The murmur of peaceful waters starts up somewhere else. Thick foliage is being crushed underfoot.

She fingers the hair on her head, which to her is stiff and dry—and she is right, it is, it is.

He doesn't insist, although he did feel an impulse rise up in his throat.

"I will stop it right there," he told himself, and he obeyed himself.

The sparse, messed-up hair on her head, her legs, that most unsightly site between her legs would soon be prodded and disturbed.

Where's peace?

The greatest feeling of satisfaction, the way to deepen the experience for her, would be not to let her legs move very far apart, or, in fact, to go ahead and let her legs do that.

She will become aware of how this maneuvering, or absence of maneuvering, can procure a beneficial result.

There are some people who cannot get.

His twitching—his very best flesh—is in her fist.

19

HE DID NOT KNOW IF HE SHOULD
BE THINKING

He did not know if he should be thinking.
I think they are going to have their dinner—
keep the meal simple. She is serving a heavy, sweet
pudding. She pours the milk. He is saying, "Just look
at this."

Out beyond, in a not so thickly wooded place, a
flying thing is buzzing around an ultrasexy flower.
Here, too, is the sloping wall of a cavernous pit, with
a post at its center—many feet long—which has been
sharpened at the exposed pole for one of us.

Suddenly, I had a comforting thought: I am not
usually as willful as I used to be.

A matchstick bursts into flame while the woman
holds the matchstick. This is the way of things.

The man is glancing at their food. He checks to

remember a skillet peach dumpling, a folded rug, or folded food.

She did not sit with him when he drank something.

He is pointing at her.

20

HIS SPIRITS WERE HIGH

He astonished her. There was flirtation. Neither of them is bored with either of them.

She wanted to keep on seeing his helike face.

So do I.

She wanted to keep on being very kind to him. She didn't think she could do this.

Out through the window, anytime of the day or night, there are any number of divinely inspired events which I have not been invited to.

She renews her strength with a silly notion, after pulling off her sock. She holds on to the sock for dear life.

"Please go back to what you were doing," he says.

Her other foot is still up inside of her sock.

Or down inside of it.

"What is this?" he says, indicating.

21

AT FIRST, SHE SAW NOTHING
UNUSUAL

Is it a door to a secret room?" he asks her.

"What do you mean?" she says.

She shuts the door to the broom closet.

This happened the day before I decided to leave them alone, before I decided to leave off pestering them.

She puts on those brand-new slippers that are not characterized by a rear opening and have an almost complete lack of heel.

She says, "You are my favorite person. How do you like that?"

She is warning him with such confidence, wondering what her words could mean.

At first, she saw nothing unusual.

A few shoots of dark hair on her belly can be seen on her belly.

The door to the kitchen stands open, where fragile porcelain, of various cherished colors, is streaked with a fricassee.

A small figure from another world needs my permission for a taste of something. I signal—to show—that this will be okay.

"Don't forget whose idea this was!" the man is saying to the woman. "Mine, you thief!"

"We can speculate," she answers.

She is . . . well, carefree.

She is nearly naked, being pulled by her arm.

That light hissing I hear when the arm of her blouse is sliding off of her is so exquisite this time that I cannot help wondering why I never paid attention to it before.

This is not anything like music, melancholy or otherwise.

This precious release cannot lull us to sleep, although I can hardly stand up or even keep sitting here any longer.

The man's trousers fell down around his ankles again, covering his footwear and accessories.

Now everything they will do must be complicated and time-consuming because he is fucking her.

She had just become very responsible. Now she wants to feel weaker, weaker, weaker, weaker.

Perhaps the secret concerning sexual intercourse, which she does not know, has made her secretive.

22

IMAGINE!

Were you here?" the man was asking of somebody.

What if he was asking me?

"I just have to know!" he was saying. "Were you here this time?"

I do not know what more to say—so I could have stopped myself from speaking.

Why don't they just live and live here? Imagine! He doesn't even have to answer the telephone!

Within a few weeks, he had told her, "Sit down."

I think it was for sex.

She pretended to sit.

He was afraid. He drank some cold beef tea. Everything about the tea was unbeatable. It was the best tea.

Why could she not leave well enough alone?

I wanted to believe that she has an elegant mind. But she just doesn't.

She watched him watch her. This is what is keeping her aroused—her pigeon-blood, cushion-shaped gemstone.

I am so proud of that ruby.

The man tries to grasp the meaning of what he should do next.

The telephone is ringing.

Even though I do adore almost any racket, I always think that this kind is tiresome.

I was wishing for my own home a thousand times.

Some of the woman's hair hung down over her face. One of his hands was on top of her head. Both of her hands were on one of her knees. They had torn the blankets and the pillows from the bed.

Then themselves.

23

SHE WILL TAKE A BIG BREATH

I found out what she was supposed to do next: behave as if she is enjoying the experience.

She says, "Thank you."

I cannot imagine saying some of the things that she brings herself to say.

"But—I don't believe it," he said. He said, "I don't believe it."

Neither one of these people is the one who gives me a reason to live on when there is no other reason. It is somebody else!

Any day this woman will be down on her back, with her knees up. She will take a big breath. She will be encouraged when he plugs up her awry anus with his straight penis.

24

DID HE STAND UP JUST TO LOOK AROUND?

Yes, I could see that there had been that hunger in her to feel herself split in half.

I do not want her to know what he is ashamed of.

On top of the toilet tank, there is a filbert, and a cherry stone lying in an openly ostentatious box inlaid with jewels. Part of a walnut is clinging to its smashed shell in the waste bin.

She has herself pressed against the door. "What are you doing? What do you think you're doing?" she is asking him.

He is sitting on the toilet with his elbows on his knees. Then he leaps up.

It is just terrible to see him this way.

But she is still curious to learn more about gentleness, about courtesy—and I do have a fondness for this place because of the stuff strewn all over it.

25

IT IS JUST SUCH AN UNPOPULAR THING TO DO

Even in this bathroom there is a skinning knife! In every nook and cranny of this cottage there is something that appeals to me.

Will she miss it here as much as I do when I go away?

Did the man stand up just to take a look about and let his thing be seen?

She says, "Wash it."

They really haven't had much privacy. But they have so much time on their hands! And I do, too!

"You take your time," a kind gent said once so sincerely as he labored to provoke me with his caresses, for heaven's sake.

A big brute stood by us to keep up our morale.

I did not think I knew either one of them. But

nearly everyone I know resembles someone I have known or someone that I know.

The men, the woman, the children are just unfamiliar enough to me so that I do not mind telling any one of them to take as long as it is necessary.

It is just such an unpopular thing to do, though, to take forever to come.

26

I COULD DO THAT

When you are inside of me, this is not unlike my reaching down into a barrel or a big pail for something which I want which is out of my reach, but the barrel needs to be knocked over onto its side.

I could do that.

I graze the back of her hand with the tail end of his penis. Somebody might think that this is true before it is true. I should have always known that I could satisfy her.

When I was confused, he poked a finger up into her vagina.

This time, at least, I am not waiting for matters to be made clear.

27

I BEND DOWN

When I sat down on top of him, having put his impressively distinct penis up inside of her, everything was what I hoped it should be.

I told him that nobody could fill her shoes.

I had to say things to her that I have never said before.

Every night I would have sat up late, by the fire, so horribly worried about this fact. But that was in the old days.

In the afternoons, if the weather is acceptable for this work, we will think even more about you.

Did I already tell you about the bugleweed that climbed up over the log?

Now the weed heads for the mossy bank, for shade which is too shady for any grass. It is twisting itself up beside a brownish material, climbing up over the log, all because I intend to bend down.

I bend down. I am hearing the rain. I am wishing you well because there is more to come.

28

YOU WILL SEE ME

You will see me not stop being a visitor who could cause a difficulty to such an extent that we would have to handle the ensuing catastrophe, which is ticklish—get some other people to try to get me to pay attention to us.

For example, my mother is a woman who believes my father is more powerful than I am.

My usual rule about building a life or a vase is that it must be slightly tapered.

Most objects require form, don't they?

Small rarities, which are strongly made, well braced, pasty, jellylike, soupy enough, or which are the correct distance apart, will increase in size.

One day, when I walked along the street, I saw my brother carrying a chair.

One of the ears of the chair and the top rail of it,

the chair, were scratched. A stile was scratched. The apron of the chair was scratched. One of the finials of the chair had broken loose, was wavering. A joining looked well joined.

My brother had the chair hoisted over his head.

I am not saying there was anything more to this since there was no weather, no water, no barren plain, no rill, no cleft, nor any hillock for as far as my eye could see, and the central peak is so far off.

My brother is somebody I am shy with, who is my idea of a friend, although I hate the nature of everything he is.

If I say that he is really my brother, then I could say nothing is wrong with me except for the aches and pains.

He put down the chair on the sidewalk.

"That's a very nice necktie," I said. "Do you always wear that necktie? You always have on a nice necktie. Is it the same necktie?"

"No, this is a different one," he said.

"You look wonderful," I said. "I can't remember you looking as good as you look."

"Fuck you," he said.

His little girl tugged on the back of his shirt. She was chattering. She—she wants to tell me everything she can think of which is more interesting than anything that you or I could ever think of.

There is a cure for everything.

29

I SHOULD BE CARRIED OFF

Considering my increasing interest in, and my knowledge of, the most distant future, I should be carried off for a rendezvous to a place that has an undulating surface, which is inconceivably swampy along the coast—to a life I might not imagine, where there can be some volcanic activity, some full understanding of human health and disease.

The largest city there, which is located in a cultural and medical center, has a great deal of quarried pink quartzite, which I know I like. There is a lake there, too, far above water level, in a sunken volcanic crater. Camellias bloom at the lakeside among live oaks, and azaleas. This is where the temperatures and the humidity have combined to produce the newest conditions.

I still intend to meet up often with you. You listen

through thick and through thin. You urge me on. I thank you. I thank you. I thank you. It is high time to give you a complicated sentence.

If you think I will never see you, you are wrong.

30

BUT IT ISN'T URGENT

I will see you!

At this time, I am staying with friends. It is difficult to get into the bathroom. My sister never says, Don't run the washing machine at all hours.

My sister, my husband, they should offer me a drink.

"Let's have a drink," my sister says.

If it had been urgent, I would have told you that it was urgent. But it isn't urgent.

My sister asked my husband if he would go to the market to get us something to consume.

He said, "Eat this."

She did not say, Could you go now?

He never went off.

No major damage to life or to property otherwise occurred. But I learned a lesson I will never forget.

31

AS IT TURNS OUT

I will encourage myself to lead a more up-to-date way of life, in a rarer atmosphere, where something in the world is really wanted or needed.

People either like me or they don't. Nobody is ever completely persuaded or enthusiastic, though.

Many of those who have thought that they enjoyed my company have not, in fact, been charmed, as it turns out.

I think that they pretend to be in heaven, which is rather romantic.

Heaven all around us, I am fond of saying.

My husband gave me something which demands something. He said, "See?"

I put it on.

He said he had paid for it.

I wear it, paying for it, too.

32

AND NOW

This is the happiest day of my life, even when I
remember this day.

I start for home.

"And now," I say to myself, "never for as long as
I live will I ever forget this happiness!"

What do you suppose? I feel I am an important
person continuing on my way to do something very
important for evermore.

It seems too strange a coincidence to be true that I
should get so distracted by you on this day, as if I had
carefully planned it that you would show up.

I confess I have always wished that you would be
my friend, even though you are a fucking dirty Jew
sort of person.

We are as friendly as I have ever been with anyone.

I appreciate how much I want you because I wish that I can appreciate it.

I talk to you very solemnly. You seem to listen, calmly, as I offer you my home, my protection, my love for the rest of my life.

I would like to let go of your arm.

33

JUST AS A JOKE

I put my lemonade on a table.

   I try to run past you, just as a joke, but you catch me up in your arms.

   After a while, you say hoarsely, "I wish I lived here."

   "But you do!" I tell you. "We have a lot to be thankful for."

   I haven't been complaining. After all, something seems to have happened.

   Did you think you would not be invited back?

34

I AM IN LOVE

You should know, if you want to come with, that
what I am going to do now is go to the bathroom down the hall.

My feet on this floor should be in my own shoes.

I am admiring the colorful roses I have put in the
dish or the cup.

I count the money. I have not gotten to the bathroom yet. I will.

I want to finish this up so I can get on with your
life.

I do not want to have anything more to do with
most of the other people.

You could be the one who is all so certain about
what somebody wants to do next, about what we
should do next, if we should appear to be going to
the bathroom next—at the same time, of course.

We should be certain. We should have no doubt.

Everything should feel natural, normal, and as if we were being swept off our feet.

Or at least mine.

Isn't this what you want?

35

IF WE ARE NOT CAREFUL

Why do you think this is?
Say something!

If we are not careful, this could go on and on. We could stay in the bathroom whenever we get there—for a while.

This is not a good time to take a shit.

Now I am beginning to get worried.

I am worried.

I want your assurance.

I want your reassurance.

Perhaps I do not know what to do next, but everyone else does.

But do you know how to do anything under these circumstances? You don't speak to me.

I close the bathroom door behind us. I appreciate the greatness of most of the articles in this room, whether we like it or not. Some of them were your idea.

The seventeenth-century pikeman is on loan from a relation.

I could tell you what I know about your possessions, because sometimes this ignites a tender feeling in both of us, I think.

Yes, there is tenderness here, and occasionally I forget why this is. Sorry.

36

ONCE I HAD TO DO WHAT I HAD
TO DO

Of all of your favorites, I used to be the prettiest one. That's the kind of person I am. I have had some difficulty conning everybody, you first of all.

You are sauntering toward me.

Are you going to express an opinion?

I am the witness when you are silent or tedious.

I am a little worried. I am getting tired. I am getting sleepy. Hurry, hurry. You have to hurry. Can you hurry?

"Here, take these, too," I say, removing a few items from the hiding place.

You ask me, "Are you quite certain?"

Would you know how to find out?

"You are inspiring," you say, politely, I suppose.

Those are my instructions.

Pretty soon, one of us will leave the bathroom.

I think you will disapprove. You will think less of me. You will not like me. You won't like me anymore. You will stop liking me, which might impair the summer.

37

PLEASE

Don't hate me when this is really all over. Do not go around saying crappy things about me.

Walking around outside, when the sunlight is brighter, we might enjoy this, don't you think?

Suddenly, a breeze will arrive, a lively breeze.

Please, this is not such a hardship to be such winsome people, because we are not in any trouble.

Returning now, to your inquiries, to your concerns, returning to anything that concerns you, you can take care of it, or just briefly consider how you could take care of it.

But briefly, it's always, I expect, too long.

38

THE EVENTS OF THE MORNING WERE
FAIRLY INTERESTING

We could talk about it. Yes, your situation is certainly more of a monstrosity than mine is. Don't you have many more reasons to die than I do?

I admit everything gets easier and easier for me— as time goes by.

I get what I want when I want it. I have been, am, will be, well served.

We did get the celery soup. It's what I'd like, you know.

The events of the morning were fairly interesting. This is my news. We were on the toilet, you realize.

39

EVERYTHING OCCURS AS PLANNED

Everything occurs as planned. I am thrilled. I do not consider it poor taste to be this proud of a pair of shoes.

The shoes I am wearing are a recollection from your childhood.

"Don't you like them?" I say.

"They're so strange," you say.

40

ANYTIME OF THE DAY OR EVENING

You have been taking advantage of some enjoy-
able moments. But you might be mistaken. Fi-
nally, you have come to believe that you should savor
life. All of this adventure of ours has used up only
about thirty-five minutes.

Time for our copulation.

I feel so amorous, but only a colossal effort has en-
titled me to feel this way.

"Please don't. Please," you beg me.

You have more than one deep, oozing starting
point, it looks like. How did this happen?

You give me a playful kick. My foot is on you.

Why don't you let me stand on you even fleetingly?

Should I remember this?

Is there any reason to remember this?

To remember you? Oh—

41

HASN'T SOMEONE DONE THIS THINKING FOR US?

Hasn't someone done this thinking for us?
    Look out!
"Sorry."
Will you get away from these discomforts? The smell of mice? The plain ordinary dirtiness of my wanting to push yours or my filthy hair around, without my having to have one tremor of sensation?

I am ardent in the afternoon.

Perhaps I am a smaller, darker person than what you had in mind.

So sorry if you are not completely happy.

Be assured this repulsive moment is coming.

It is not safely past.

Nor passed.

42

THIS TIME YOU SAY NO

You just want to be here with me.

The temperature of the room is cool. I want to pet you, but not your private part. I would not touch it with a fork.

You would think if I could tolerate the bedside clock that I could bind up your parcel with the cord!

They did not know why I felt this way.

You saw my nakedness. You had a great deal to worry about, even if I had made much of bathing daily. Yet you treated me courteously. You told me that you wanted me to remain in good cheer.

I was given a washing, which nearly fortified me. I was fed the right foods. Let me tell you it will take much more strength to stop my pleasure in the nick of time than what I now have.

I forget—where did you say came from?

No, come.

Why don't you answer me?

Here is my solution that could help you anytime anywhere. Here is my advice, even though many of you consider me to be unclean.

Sweetness! Something wonderful will happen to you, which will make me happy!

They can keep remembering this—even if we do not.

43

WE COULD FIX AN EGG

I could do something so that you and I would not be invited back.

You are better-looking than I am, better prepared, better behaved.

I do not like these men as much as I know I am supposed to.

I am so glad there are no little girls here. I would loathe it if there were little girls here. Older women give me that sense that I have value, but little girls make me feel like shit.

We could fix an egg.

Don't keep saying that! I don't agree. Don't tell me what to do!

44

A NECESSITY ARISES

I am the one who tells you what to think.
We are very similar to people who stay together who do not really love each other but who want to love each other so much.

A necessity arises which has caused both of us to tremble all over. We—nobody could say why this is.

We could give this necessity the wretched synopsis it deserves: The Story of Our Lives.

One never knows, not for a thousand years, the way to speak to a woman such as I am, one who wears such footwear, who goes into the courtyard, who reposes at the fire, who undertakes the tasks— the tufts, the hollows—it is indescribable.

What if she even knew what she was doing when she cooked almost every vegetable available? Fruit is what she claims she likes. The liar.

The sounds on the roof could be scuffling, if it is a good night. We hear its goodness.

Some human beings do not hurt people, or damage property. They do not intensely glow, or become indivisible by merely looking at you.

To learn more about them, people should use you.

Diane Williams is coeditor of *StoryQuarterly*.

A NOTE ON THE TYPE

The text of this book was set in Sabon.

Composed by North Market Street Graphics,
Lancaster, Pennsylvania
Printed and bound by Berryville Graphics,
Berryville, Virginia
Designed by Virginia Tan